Agapanthus Hum and the Eyeglasses

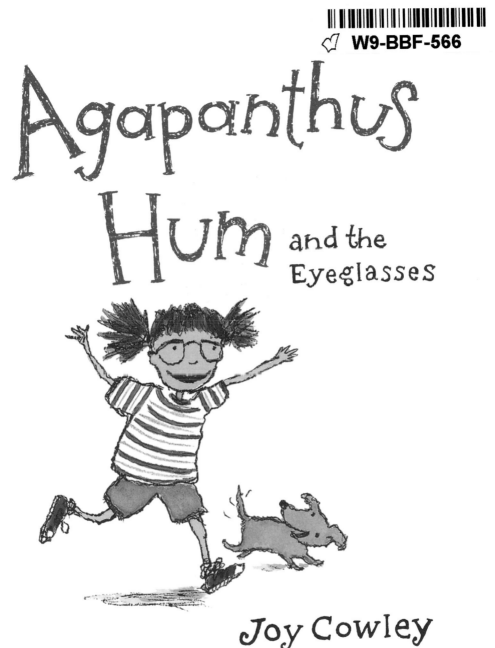

Joy Cowley

author of Mrs. Wishy-Washy

Pictures by Jennifer Plecas

PUFFIN BOOKS

PUFFIN BOOKS
Published by the Penguin Group
Penguin Putnam Books for Young Readers, 345 Hudson Street, New York, New York 10014, U.S.A.
Penguin Books Ltd, 27 Wrights Lane, London W8 5TZ, England
Penguin Books Australia Ltd, Ringwood, Victoria, Australia
Penguin Books Canada Ltd, 10 Alcorn Avenue, Toronto, Ontario, Canada M4V 3B2
Penguin Books (N.Z.) Ltd, 182-190 Wairau Road, Auckland 10, New Zealand
Penguin Books Ltd, Registered Offices: Harmondsworth, Middlesex, England

First published in the United States of America by Philomel Books,
a division of Penguin Putnam Books for Young Readers, 1999
Published by Puffin Books, a division of Penguin Putnam Books for Young Readers, 2001

1 3 5 7 9 10 8 6 4 2

Text copyright © Joy Cowley, 1999
Illustrations copyright © Jennifer Plecas, 1999
All rights reserved

THE LIBRARY OF CONGRESS HAS CATALOGED THE PHILOMEL EDITION AS FOLLOWS:
Cowley, Joy.
Agapanthus Hum and the eyeglasses /
illustrated by Jennifer Plecas.
p.   cm.
Summary: Agapanthus struggles to do handstands and other acrobatic tricks while wearing
her eyeglasses, which have a tendency to fall off as she cavorts about.
[1. Eyeglasses—Fiction. 2. Acrobats—Fiction.] I. Plecas, Jennifer, ill. II. Title.
PZ7.C8375Ag 1999 [E]—dc21 97-38404 CIP AC ISBN 0-399-23211-7

This edition ISBN 0-698-11883-9
Puffin® and Easy-to-Read® are registered trademarks of Penguin Putnam Inc.

Printed in Hong Kong
Set in Goudy Old Style

Reading Level 3

Table of Contents

Chapter One

Agapanthus Hum had tunes inside her,
tunes for running and whirling,
tunes for dancing in the wind,
tunes that bubbled toothpaste
and gurgled lemonade.

"Agapanthus," said good little Mommy,
"You are just like a music box."

That was very true.

The moment Agapanthus woke up,

a humming started inside her.

It buzzed and buzzed around her head

until it found a way out through her nose.

Good little Daddy said she was called Hum
because she was such a whizzer,
humming and whizzing
like a button on a string.

One day good little Daddy said,
"Slow down, honey. If you rush so much
there could be another you-know-what."
He meant accident but was too kind to say so.

3

"People who wear eyeglasses
have to be careful, Agapanthus,"
said good little Mommy.

"The makers of eyeglasses
are not very kind
to the whizzers and rushers
of this world,"
said good little Daddy.

"Not kind like
you and Mommy,"
said Agapanthus Hum,
and she ran at them
with such big hugs
that her glasses came off
and swung from one ear.

"Oops," she said.

Good little Mommy took the eyeglasses.
With a tissue, she wiped off smudges
of toothpaste and peanut butter.

5

"I will be very careful,"
said Agapanthus Hum. "I will not twirl.
I will not rush or whizz.
I will not lose my glasses!"

Good little Mommy laughed
and gave her a kiss.
"Agapanthus Hum, we love you."

Chapter Two

Clean glasses made the garden look
as sharp as a tune played on a fiddle.
Agapanthus twirled, but only a little.
She did a butterfly hum
on the face of a pink rose.

She whizzed, but not much,
around the oak tree.
She pressed her hands on a lawn
as soft as baby hair.
But then she forgot and kicked
both feet up in a handstand
to look at her world upside down.

"I can stand on my hands!" she cried.
"Mommy! Daddy! Come and see."

They came running from the house.
"Agapanthus!" called Daddy
in his wait-a-minute voice.

But Agapanthus did not hear.
She was kicking her feet in the air
and shouting, "Look at me!"

Then she wobbled,
and her shout became a grunt.
Her eyeglasses slipped off her nose
and dropped right onto the grass.

"Oops," cried Agapanthus
and she crashed on top of them.

Her hum puffed out
like a birthday candle,
and her head went quiet.
She felt about for the glasses,
then she got a funny feeling.

She was sitting on them!
Good little Daddy and good little Mommy
came running across the grass.
"Are you hurt, honey?" they said.

Agapanthus could not say a word.
Good little Daddy took the glasses.
"All is not lost, Agapanthus Hum,
we can do some fixing."

Chapter Three

Good little Mommy said,
"I have a new box of tissues.
You can cry all you want."

But Agapanthus did not want to cry.
Her glasses could be mended!
A tune got up and flew
around her head.
It was a busy tune for fixing things.

Good little Mommy
put the glasses
in a sink
of hot water
and bent them
back into shape.

Good little Daddy got a baby screwdriver
and a screw no bigger than a turnip seed,
and put the arm back on.

"They are not as good as new," he said.
"But they will be okay."

Agapanthus put on her glasses.
"I will be very,
very, very, very,
very, very careful,"
she said.

Good little Mommy said,
"That was a great handstand, Agapanthus.
You looked just like an acrobat."
"An acrobat!" cried Agapanthus Hum.
"Really and truly?"

"Exactly like an acrobat,"
said good little Daddy.

Chapter Four

Agapanthus had a brown paper bag.
She cut two holes in it
so that she could see.
Then she put the paper bag
over her head.

16

She went outside,
humming her clever song.
The tune rattled the paper bag
and made it tickle her nose.
She could not see much
through thc holes
but she could see the grass.

Now, if she did a handstand
and her glasses came off,
they would drop
into the paper bag
and be safe.

She put her hands
down on the grass
and kicked her feet in the air.
The glasses stayed on her nose,
but the paper bag fell off.

"Oh, pickles!" said Agapanthus Hum.

Good little Mommy
came out of the house.
"Agapanthus,
do you know
a strange thing?
I have never seen acrobats
wearing eyeglasses.
What do you think they do with them?"

"I don't know." Agapanthus hummed.

"I think an acrobat puts her glasses
in her mother's pocket
until she is finished
all that twirling and tumbling,"
said good little Mommy.

"That's what I can do!" said Agapanthus,
taking her glasses off her nose
and putting them in her mother's pocket.

For the rest of the afternoon
Agapanthus was a beautiful acrobat
humming an upside-down tune.
By the time she put her glasses back on
she could walk four steps on her hands.

Chapter Five

Good little Daddy and good little Mommy
said, "There is an acrobat show in town."
Would Agapanthus like to go to it?

Agapanthus was so pleased
that when she opened her mouth,
her hum burst into a song.

Good little Mommy helped her
to get dressed in her best white frock.
Agapanthus helped good little Mommy
to get ready for the show.

She saw a string of blue beads
in good little Mommy's drawer.
But the drawer slammed shut
as she pulled the beads out,
and the string broke.

Beads went everywhere,
like blue hailstones.

"What a lucky thing!"
said good little Mommy.
"If that had happened at the show
I would never have found them all."

Agapanthus said to good little Mommy,
"You can wear my necklace,
the one with a clown on it.
It's a real acrobat necklace."

"Why, thank you, Agapanthus Hum,"
said good little Mommy.
"That is very kind of you."

Chapter Six

The acrobat show was in a tent.
While they were waiting
for the show to begin,
good little Daddy got strawberry ice cream
for Agapanthus Hum.

Agapanthus was humming
a topsy-turvy acrobat song
and did not see the ice cream
dripping all the way down her arm!
She tried to lick it off,
but her tongue would not go
as far as her elbow.

When she put her arm down,
her elbow stuck to her dress.

Loud music filled the tent.

People began to clap.

The acrobats came twirling out,

dressed in red and silver.

They flipped forward

and walked on their hands.

They rolled up into the air.

They did cartwheels on the ground.

They stood on each other's shoulders
and jumped high off a teeter-totter.

Agapanthus forgot her ice cream.

She even forgot to hum.

She was a famous acrobat.

She had acrobat arms

and acrobat legs

and they were getting all whizzy

wanting to do acrobat things.

Everyone went, "Ooooooooooo!"

A beautiful lady with white tights jumped

from one swing to another swing.

She waved.

"I am going to do that,"
Agapanthus Hum said to good little Daddy.
"I am going to be just like her."

Good little Daddy smiled and said,
"Let me take that messy old ice cream."

Chapter Seven

After the acrobat show,
good little Mommy and good little Daddy
looked for some water
to wash the ice cream
off Agapanthus—off her cheeks and nose,
her arms and legs,
and her pretty white dress.

They could not find any water.

There were some trailers
at the back of the tent.
A lady in a white robe
sat in a chair, reading a book.
She was wearing eyeglasses
that were a bit lopsided,
just like the eyeglasses
of Agapanthus Hum.

"Excuse me," said good little Mommy.
"May we please have some water?"

"Sure thing," said the lady.
She got up and went into the trailer.
Under her robe the lady was wearing
white tights!

"It's her! It's her!" cried Agapanthus,
whirling and whirling.
"It's the beautiful lady on the swing."

The lady came out with a wet cloth
and a fluffy dry towel.

She helped Agapanthus
to wash the sticky ice cream
off her cheeks and nose,

her hands and arms,

and her white dress.

"They don't make ice cream cones
like they used to," said the beautiful lady.

There was so much whizz in Agapanthus
she could not keep still for a moment.
She said to the lady with the white tights,
"Where do you put your eyeglasses
when you are swinging on your swing?"

The lady looked at good little Mommy
and good little Daddy.

"We think you give your glasses
to your mother," said good little Mommy.

"Well, how did you find that out?"
laughed the beautiful lady.
"It's what all the best acrobats do."

"I know, I know!" cried Agapanthus,
and then, unable to stop herself,
she put her hands on the ground
and kicked up her heels.

Oops!

But it was all right
because the lady reached down
and caught the eyeglasses
of Agapanthus Hum.
Just in time.